Ready or Not, Here Comes SCOUT!

by **Jill Abramson** *and* **Jane O'Connor**

illustrated by **Deborah Melmon**

Viking

An Imprint of Penguin Group (USA) Inc.

HELLO! My name is Scout, and this is Baby, my best friend in the world. We are both puppies, only I'm real and Baby isn't.

We do everything together.

Baby sure loves a good mud bath.

Ooh ooh! Guess what!

Today we're going to the park, because I'm big enough now for real friends. My human thinks we should leave Baby home, because she might get lost.

No way! Not a chance!

Where I go, Baby goes too.

I've never seen so many dogs! I'm going to be friends with all of them! Every single one.

DOG PARK

HOURS:
8am to Dusk

Ooh ooh! A puppy pool. And it looks like there's room for one more.

Ready or not . . . here I come!

Uh oh! It turns out not all dogs like splashing.
I never knew that.

Ooh ooh! See those two dogs playing tug-of-war? I know a game that's way more fun.

Ready or not . . . here I come!

I grab the rope away. Chase me! Chase me!

What? I have to give back the rope?
How come? I was just trying to be friends.

Ooh ooh! Isn't that little bitty dog the cutest thing ever!
I give her a great big kiss—SMOOCH!—to show how
much I like her. But she doesn't kiss me back.

When it's time to go home,
I still have only one friend—Baby.

My human takes Baby and me back to the park the next day . . . and the next. I watch how friends play with each other.

Now I wade in the pool with Buddy and Arrow. I don't splash.

I wait till Linda wants to play tug-of-war with me.

I am gentle with Petunia.

I even let my friends play with Baby.

Wow! See how popular I am now!

One day a new dog comes to the park.

His name is Taco. All he does is play fetch with his human.

Taco sure looks like he needs a friend.

Ready or not . . . here I come!

Hold on a second! Something's wrong.

The hairs on Taco's back stand up.
Taco growls and shows his teeth.

I run away. Poor Baby is terrified. She insists on going home—right NOW!

After that, Baby and I won't go to the park.
We never want to see Taco again.

Dogs that look like Taco scare us—
even dogs on TV.

It's been so long since I've seen my friends.
I bet they miss me terribly.

I feel awfully bad for them. . . . Maybe I should go back.

Ooh ooh! What a welcome I get!

Baby and I are careful to stay far away from Taco.
I play all afternoon with my friends. I am practically
out of my mind with happiness!

My human says it's almost time to go home.

But where is Baby?

Baby? *Baby!*

Oh no! Baby is missing!

I search everywhere for her.
I am nearly out of my mind with worry!

You'll never guess who finds Baby . . . Taco!
Baby was taking a mud bath!

Taco drops Baby near me. That means I can pick her up.

As soon as I do, Taco runs away.

All my friends are calling to me. There's
a game of tag. I wish Taco would play
too. Maybe one day he will want to.
Me, I'm ready to play *now*!

12-12-3
B2+ 1599/12.71

To Henry—J.A.

To Arrow and the late, great Lucky—J.O'C.

For Mack, who makes sure I get to the dog park every day.—D.M.

🐕

Viking
Published by the Penguin Group
Penguin Young Readers Group, 345 Hudson Street, New York, New York 10014, U.S.A.
Penguin Group (Canada), 90 Eglinton Avenue East, Suite 700, Toronto, Ontario, Canada M4P 2Y3 (a division of Pearson Penguin Canada Inc.)
Penguin Books Ltd, 80 Strand, London WC2R 0RL, England
Penguin Ireland, 25 St Stephen's Green, Dublin 2, Ireland (a division of Penguin Books Ltd)
Penguin Group (Australia), 250 Camberwell Road, Camberwell, Victoria 3124, Australia (a division of Pearson Australia Group Pty Ltd)
Penguin Books India Pvt Ltd, 11 Community Centre, Panchsheel Park, New Delhi – 110 017, India
Penguin Group (NZ), 67 Apollo Drive, Rosedale, Auckland 0632, New Zealand (a division of Pearson New Zealand Ltd.)
Penguin Books (South Africa) (Pty) Ltd, 24 Sturdee Avenue, Rosebank, Johannesburg 2196, South Africa

Penguin Books Ltd, Registered Offices: 80 Strand, London WC2R 0RL, England

First published in the United States of America by Viking, a division of Penguin Young Readers Group, 2012

1   3   5   7   9   10   8   6   4   2

Text copyright © Jill Abramson and Jane O'Connor, 2012
Illustrations copyright © Deborah Melmon, 2012
All rights reserved

LIBRARY OF CONGRESS CATALOGING-IN-PUBLICATION DATA
Jill Abramson and Jane O'Connor ; illustrated by Deborah Melmon.
p. cm.
Summary: Scout, a rambunctious puppy, proves overeager to make friends on her first visit to the park but learns,
over time, how to get along well with the other dogs there.
ISBN 978-0-670-01441-5 (hardback)
1. Golden retriever—Juvenile fiction. [1. Golden retriever—Fiction. 2. Dogs—Fiction. 3. Animals—Infancy—Fiction.] I. O'Connor, Jane.
II. Melmon, Deborah, ill. III. Title.
PZ10.3.A11Re 2012   [E]—dc23   2012001295

Manufactured in China   Set in Bodoni Six   Book design by Nancy Brennan
The art for this book was created with pencil and watercolor on 100 percent rag paper and manipulated in Photoshop.

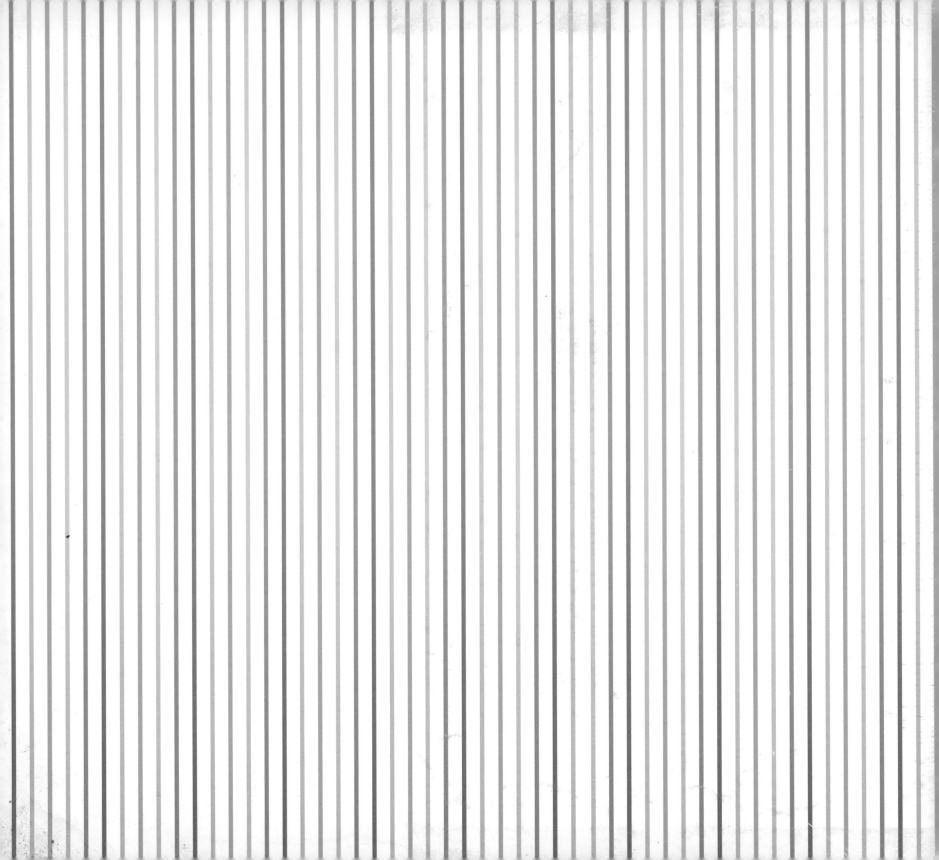